Published in the United States 2004 by Dutton Children's Books,
a division of Penguin Young Readers Group
345 Hudson Street, New York, New York 10014
www.penguin.com

Originally published in Great Britain 1997 and revised 2003 by Egmont Books, London
Printed in Malaysia · First American Edition
ISBN 0-525-47325-4
3 5 7 9 10 8 6 4 2

Winnie-the-Pooh
Baby Days

INSPIRED BY **A. A. Milne**

ILLUSTRATIONS BY **Ernest H. Shepard**

DUTTON CHILDREN'S BOOKS · NEW YORK

Contents

Waiting for Baby

Due date

....

Choice of names for baby

....

....

....

....

....

Mother's name

....

Father's name

....

How Mother and Father met

....

....

....

Prenatal scan   Date.................................

Now it happened that Kanga had felt rather motherly that morning, and Wanting to Count Things—like Roo's vests, and how many pieces of soap there were left, and the two clean spots in Tigger's feeder; so she sent them out with a packet of watercress sandwiches and a packet of extract-of-malt sandwiches for Tigger.

Feelings about having a baby

....

....

....

....

....

....

*When I first heard his name, I said, just as
you are going to say, "But I thought he was a boy?"
"So did I," said Christopher Robin.
"Then you can't call him Winnie?"
"I don't."
"But you said—"
"He's Winnie-ther-Pooh.
Don't you know what 'ther' means?"*

Photograph

Mother/Father

Baby's Birth

Baby was born on   month   day   year

....

Time of birth

....

Place of birth

....

Who was present at the birth

....

"When you wake up in the morning, Pooh," said Piglet at last, "what's the first thing you say to yourself?"
"What's for breakfast?" said Pooh.
"What do you say, Piglet?"
"I say, I wonder what's going to happen exciting today?" said Piglet.
Pooh nodded thoughtfully.
"It's the same thing," he said.

Weight at birth

....

Length at birth

....

Color of eyes

....

Color of hair

....

Name of doctor

....

Name of midwife

....

Very first photograph of baby

Description of the birth

....

....

....

....

....

....

....

....

....

Things to Remember

Handprint

Footprint

Identity tag from hospital

"I think—" began Piglet nervously.
"Don't," said Eeyore.
"I think Violets are rather nice,"
said Piglet. And he laid his bunch in
front of Eeyore and scampered off.

Pressed flowers

Cards and gifts from

Date

Visitors

....

....

....

....

....

Who sent flowers

....

....

....

....

....

....

*Newspaper Clippings
and Cards*

Birth Announcements

Baby's First Day

Distinctive features

....

....

Sign of the zodiac

....

Weather on this day

....

....

No one can tell me,
　　Nobody knows,
Where the wind comes from,
　　Where the wind goes.

It's flying from somewhere
　　As fast as it can,
I couldn't keep up with it,
　　Not if I ran.

But if I stopped holding
　　The string of my kite,
It would blow with the wind
　　For a day and a night.

And then when I found it,
　　Wherever it blew,
I should know that the wind
　　Had been going there too.

So then I could tell them
　　Where the wind goes . . .
But where the wind comes from
　　Nobody knows.

On This Day

Famous events in history that happened on this date

....

....

....

....

....

Famous people born on this day

....

....

....

....

No. 1 song on the music charts

....

"Are you," he said, "by any chance
His Majesty the King of France?"
The other answered, "I am that,"
Bowed stiffly, and removed his hat;
Then said, "Excuse me," with an air,
"But is it Mr. Edward Bear?"

And Teddy, bending very low,
Replied politely, "Even so!"

Front Page of the Newspaper Today

Coming Home

Baby came home on

....

Address of family home

....

....

....

Who was there to welcome baby?

....

....

....

....

On the first night home, baby fell asleep at

.... a.m./p.m.

.... a.m./p.m.

Baby awoke at

.... a.m./p.m.

.... a.m./p.m.

Photograph

Baby's first night at home

Settling Down

Baby's feeding times

....

....

Breast or bottle?

....

Sleeping times

....

Wakeful times

....

Favorite sleeping position

....

Mother's feelings

....

....

....

 Then Tigger looked up at the ceiling, and closed his eyes, and his tongue went round and round his chops, in case he had left any outside, and a peaceful smile came over his face as he said, "So that's what Tiggers like!"

Father's feelings

....

....

....

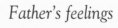

Naming Baby

Pooh

Now this bear's name is Winnie, which shows what a good name for bears it is, but the funny thing is that we can't remember whether Winnie is called after Pooh, or Pooh after Winnie. We did know once, but we have forgotten.

Baby's name

....

Date of christening or Name Day celebrations

....

Baby wore

....

Godparents

....

....

....

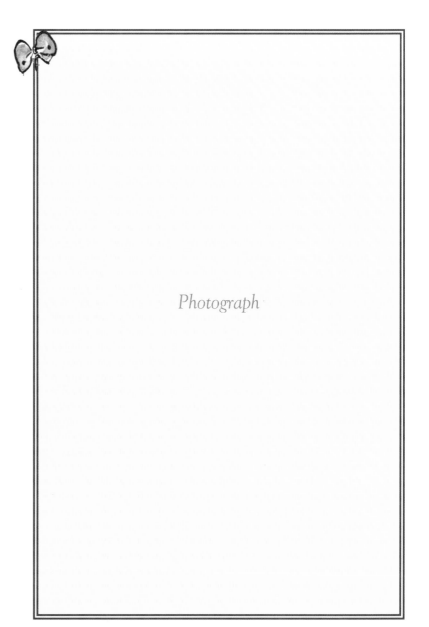

Photograph

Baby's Name Day

Baby's name means

....

Name was chosen by

....

Reason for choosing name

....

....

Gifts received

....

....

....

....

....

....

....

Photograph

Name Day celebration

Family Tree

Family Photograph

Next to his house was a piece of broken board which had:
"TRESPASSERS W" on it. When Christopher Robin asked
the Piglet what it meant, he said it was his grandfather's
name, and had been in the family for a long time.

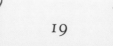

MOTHER'S SIDE

Great-grandmother

....

Great-grandfather

....

Grandmother

....

Grandfather

....

Baby's mother

....

FATHER'S SIDE

Great-grandmother

....

Great-grandfather

....

Grandmother

....

Grandfather

....

Baby's father

....

Baby's sisters

....

....

....

Baby's brothers

....

....

....

Baby's Progress

Photograph

Date ....

Wakes up at

....

Bathtime

....

Mealtimes

....

....

Goes to sleep at

....

Sometimes Winnie-the-Pooh likes a game of some sort when he comes downstairs, and sometimes he likes to sit quietly in front of the fire and listen to a story. . . .

How baby has changed

....

....

....

....

....

Favorite activities

....

....

....

....

....

Describe baby's first weeks

....

....

....

....

Bathtime

Does baby like bathtime?

....

Favorite bath toys

....

Favorite bath games

....

....

First bath at home

....

First time in the big bathtub

....

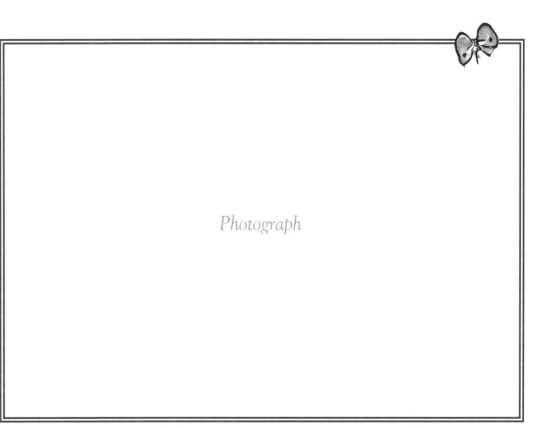

Photograph

Baby's bathtime

Bedtime

Sleeping times

....

....

First slept through the night

....

What helps baby get to sleep

....

....

Favorite bedtime toys

....

....

Favorite bedtime stories

....

....

Favorite lullabies

....

....

Binker's brave as lions when we're running in the park;
Binker's brave as tigers when we're lying in the dark;
Binker's brave as elephants. He never, never cries . . .
Except (like other people) when the soap gets in his eyes.

Mealtimes

Weaned from the breast/bottle on

....

The first time baby

ate pureed food

....

ate solid food

....

used fingers

....

held a spoon

....

sat in a high chair

....

drank from a cup with help

....

drank from a cup alone

....

ate a complete meal

....

Pooh put the cloth back on the table, and he put a large honey-pot on the cloth, and they sat down to breakfast. And as soon as they sat down, Tigger took a large mouthful of honey . . . and he looked up at the ceiling with his head on one side, and made exploring noises with his tongue, and considering noises, and what-have-we-got-here noises . . . and then he said in a very decided voice: "Tiggers don't like honey."

Photograph

Favorite foods

....

....

....

Photograph

Baby eating

Foods disliked

....

....

Immunization details

Vaccine   Age   Date

....

....

....

....

Eyesight test

....

Hearing test

....

Childhood illnesses   Date

....

....

Allergies

....

Blood type

....

Pediatrician

....

Telephone number

....

"I don't think Roo had better come," he said. "Not today."
"Why not?" said Roo, who wasn't supposed to be listening.
"Nasty cold day," said Rabbit, shaking his head. "And you were coughing this morning."
"How do you know?" asked Roo indignantly.
"Oh, Roo, you never told me," said Kanga reproachfully.
"It was a biscuit cough," said Roo, "not one you tell about."

Teething

A baby cuts twenty primary teeth from about six months old to two years old. The appearance of the first tooth is a milestone in a baby's life, although it can cause a great deal of discomfort. Some babies find chewing on a teething ring soothes the gums and helps lessen the pain. These first teeth begin to be replaced with permanent teeth when the child is about six years old.

Date of first tooth

....

Date of second tooth

....

Date of third tooth

....

Date of fourth tooth

....

Date of fifth tooth

....

Date of sixth tooth

....

Date of seventh tooth

....

Date of eighth tooth

....

Date of ninth tooth

....

Date of tenth tooth

....

Binker isn't greedy, but he does like things to eat,
So I have to say to people when they're giving me a sweet,
"Oh, Binker wants a chocolate, so could you give me two?"
And then I eat it for him, 'cos his teeth are rather new.

27

Growing

Age	Weight	Length/Height
One month	....	....
Two months	....	....
Three months	....	....
Four months	....	....
Five months	....	....
Six months	....	....
Seven months	....	....
Eight months	....	....
Nine months	....	....
Ten months	....	....
Eleven months	....	....
Twelve months	....	....

What shall we do about poor little Tigger?
If he never eats nothing he'll never get bigger.
But whatever his weight in pounds, shillings, and ounces,
He always seems bigger because of his bounces.

Photograph

Photograph

Baby at .... *months*

Baby at .... *months*

"He's quite big enough anyhow," said Piglet.
"He isn't really very big."
"Well, he seems so."

Going Out

First outing in carriage or stroller

....

First outings by

car ....

train ....

bus ....

Special outings with

grandparents

....

....

relatives

....

....

friends

....

....

....

....

Photograph

Baby on an outing to 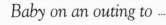...

First Vacation

First vacation

....

Traveled by

....

Destination

....

Favorite activity

....

Favorite outings

....

....

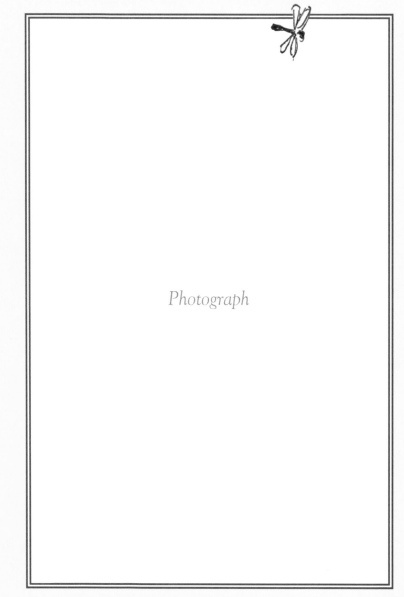

Photograph

"Christopher Robin and I are going for a Short Walk,"
he said, "not a Jostle. If he likes to bring Pooh and Piglet
with him, I shall be glad of their company, but one must
be able to Breathe."

Baby on vacation in ....

Favorite vacation memories

....

....

First Christmas

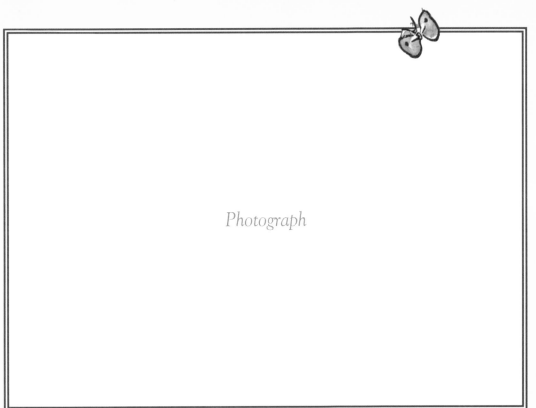

Photograph

Baby's first Christmas

"I'm very glad," said Pooh happily, "that I thought of giving you a Useful Pot to put things in."
"I'm very glad," said Piglet happily, "that I thought of giving you Something to put in a Useful Pot."
But Eeyore wasn't listening. He was taking the balloon out, and putting it back again, as happy as could be. . . .

Description of Christmas Eve

....

....

....

Where it was spent

....

Who it was spent with

....

....

....

Where Christmas Day was spent

....

Who it was spent with

....

....

....

Your present to baby

....

Description of Christmas Day

....

Gifts received   from

....

....

....

....

....

....

....

....

....

....

....

....

....

....

....

....

First Birthday

Date

....

How it was celebrated

....

....

....

Who was there

....

....

....

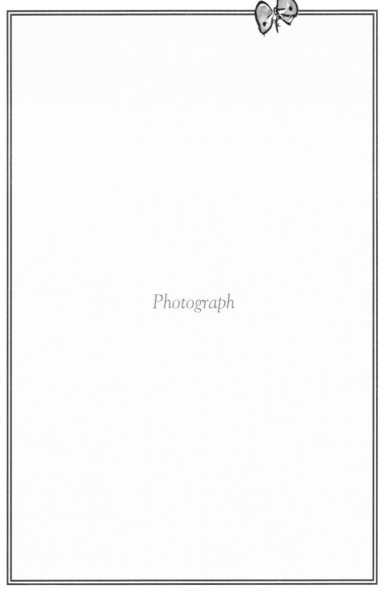

Photograph

First birthday

Where it was spent

....

Description of cake

....

....

What baby wore

....

....

Gifts received   from

....

....

....

....

Piglet had gone back to his own house to get Eeyore's balloon. He held it very tightly against himself, so that it shouldn't blow away, and he ran as fast as he could so as to get to Eeyore before Pooh did; for he thought that he would like to be the first one to give a present, just as if he had thought of it without being told by anybody.

Your present

....

Taking Steps

Photograph

Crawling .... (date)

Photograph

Holding on .... (date)

Photograph

Standing up .... (date)

Photograph

First steps without help .... (date)

First Words

First sounds   *Date*   *Favorite books*

....

....

....

First words

....

....

....

Binker's always talking, 'cos I'm teaching him to speak:
He sometimes likes to do it in a funny sort of squeak,
And he sometimes likes to do it in a hoodling sort of roar . . .
And I have to do it for him 'cos his throat is rather sore.

First Events

Focused eyes

Smiled

Sucked thumb or pacifier

Slept through the night

Held head up

Played with hands

Played with feet

Clapped hands

Grasped an object

O Timothy Tim
   Has ten pink toes,
   And ten pink toes
Has Timothy Tim.
They go with him
   Wherever he goes,
   And wherever he goes
They go with him.

O Timothy Tim
   Has two blue eyes,
   And two blue eyes
Has Timothy Tim.
They cry with him
   Whenever he cries,
   And whenever he cries,
They cry with him.

Gurgled

Laughed

Copied noises

Said "Mama"

Said "Dada"

Spoke first words

Made animal noises

Rolled over

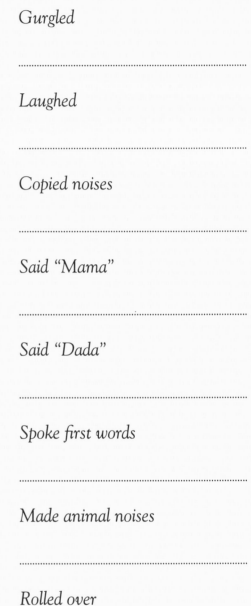

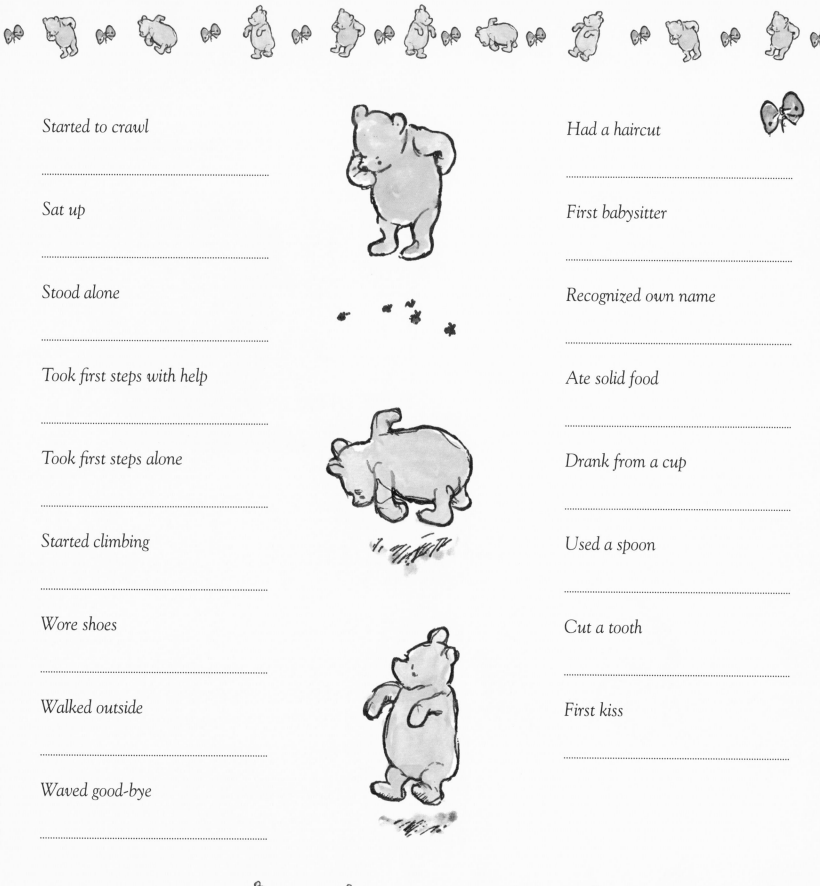

Started to crawl

....

Sat up

....

Stood alone

....

Took first steps with help

....

Took first steps alone

....

Started climbing

....

Wore shoes

....

Walked outside

....

Waved good-bye

....

Had a haircut

....

First babysitter

....

Recognized own name

....

Ate solid food

....

Drank from a cup

....

Used a spoon

....

Cut a tooth

....

First kiss

....

Favorite Things

Baby's favorite:

Toys

....

....

Games

....

....

Activities

....

....

Songs and nursery rhymes

....

....

Pictures

....

....

Blanket

....

Books

....

....

Stuffed animals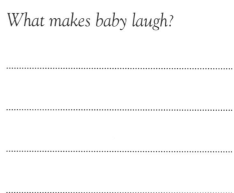

....

....

People

....

....

....

Animals

....

....

Sounds

....

....

Music

....

....

"What do you like doing best in the world, Pooh?"
"Well," said Pooh, "what I like best—" and then he had to stop and think.
Because although Eating Honey was a very good thing to do, there was a
moment just before you began to eat it which was better than when you were,
but he didn't know what it was called. And then he thought that being with
Christopher Robin was a very good thing to do, and having Piglet near was
a very friendly thing to have.

What makes baby laugh?

....

....

....

....

Special Memories

Looking back on the first year of your baby's life, you may want to record some special moments.

First friends

....

....

....

Special things to remember

....

....

....

....

....

....

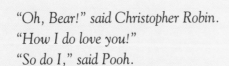

Special Photograph

Date ....

"Oh, Bear!" said Christopher Robin.
"How I do love you!"
"So do I," said Pooh.

Funny things to remember

....

....

....

....

....

Photograph

Baby's friends

The Future

Plans for the future

....

....

....

"Do you know what A means, little Piglet?"
"No, Eeyore, I don't."
"It means Learning, it means Education, it means all the things that you and Pooh haven't got. That's what A means."
"Oh," said Piglet again. "I mean, does it?" he explained quickly.

Possible preschools

....

....

....

....

Baby's personality

....

....

....

....

....

....

Scrapbook

What's become of John boy?
    Nothing at all,
He played with his skipping rope,
    He played with his ball.
He ran after butterflies,
    Blue ones and red;
He did a hundred happy things—
    And then went to bed.

Scrapbook

When I was One,
I had just begun.

When I was Two,
I was nearly new.

When I was Three,
I was hardly Me.

When I was Four,
I was not much more.

When I was Five,
I was just alive.

But now I am Six, I'm as clever as clever.
So I think I'll be six now for ever and ever.